WILD LIVES

WALKING WITH WOLVES

NICK ARNOLD

ILLUSTRATED BY JANE COPE

SCHOLASTIC

For Tom, our wonderful son!
Jane Cope

Scholastic Children's Books,
Commonwealth House, 1–19 New Oxford Street,
London WC1A 1NU, UK

A division of Scholastic Ltd
London – New York – Toronto – Sydney – Auckland
Mexico City – New Delhi – Hong Kong

Published in the UK by Scholastic Ltd, 2004

ISBN 0 439 96313 3

Printed and bound by Nørhaven Paperback A/S, Denmark
Cover image supplied by NHPA Limited.

2 4 6 8 10 9 7 5 3 1

CONTENTS

WILDWATCH CALLING ALL TEACHERS!

FANCY A WALK ON THE WILD SIDE?

If you're wild about wolves ... Wildwatch wants to hear from you! We're after a fearless teacher to watch grey wolves in the USA. Your job will be to keep a diary about a young wolf.

❏ *Enjoy lots of wolf action*
❏ *Excitement and adventure guaranteed*
❏ *Enjoy the stunning scenery of Yellowstone Park*
❏ *Excellent pay, plus expenses, including travel*
❏ *Your diary will be published by Wildwatch!*

DON'T DELAY – APPLY TODAY!

The young girl peered fearfully over her shoulder. She felt sure she had seen something in the dark, snowy forest. But what? She was cold and alone and far from home. She began to hurry through the snow, but just then a howl broke *the silence of the night. Then came more howls and deep-throated growls…*

Hungry, yellow-orange eyes shone amongst the black tree trunks. Big, sharp jaws began to snarl. The creatures longed to tear the girl's flesh and drink her blood until it dripped from their fangs. Silently, stealthily, the huge wolves crept closer. The girl screamed…

"WHAT RUBBISH!" I snapped, switching off the TV. The wolves in the film were stupid, movie monsters. I wanted to see *real* wolves – the animals I'd watched last summer.

With a cross sigh, I flopped on to the bouncy bed in Bob Fletcher's guest room and gazed at the lovely wolf photo propped up on the table next to me. As I looked at the picture, my mind went back to that first day in Yellowstone Park…

But hold on – I haven't introduced myself! My name's Willow Lane (yes, I know it sounds like a leafy road – you can blame my parents for that) and I'm a teacher at Crabtree School. If you saw me in the street, you wouldn't give me a second glance. I'm a small 25-year-old with mousy hair, a freckly nose and glasses.

THIS IS ME

I don't look the outdoor type, but I've always dreamt of having a BIG adventure. So when I saw the Wildwatch advert early last year it spoke to me, it really did... You see, I love wolves, and I decided to get away from  school and experience the excitement of the wild.

But I found more than adventure in Yellowstone Park. Something far more special. This is my story...

ALONE IN THE WILD

May 26

Aoooowwww! Somewhere outside my tent a wolf was howling. It was my first night in Yellowstone Park, and I was all by myself. I began to panic.

"They don't kill people, they don't kill people!" I repeated to myself through gritted teeth. I'd made sure I knew that before I'd agreed to stay.

Another eerie howl rang out; this time closer. The hairs on the back of my neck stood up. I nearly screamed. All at once I didn't feel so adventurous. Was I really up to the challenge of wolf-watching?

SHIVER! SHAKE!

I took a deep breath and tried to pull myself together. "Don't be silly, Willow!" I said to myself. "Just try to sleep." It had been a long, tiring day and I felt annoyed because things hadn't gone to plan.

My morning had started at the Flag Ranch Motel. I'd been staying there since flying to the States two days earlier. At 8 am I was collected by a park ranger. In his wide-brimmed hat and breeches he looked like something out of a Yogi Bear cartoon.

LARRY

"Hi – you must be Robert Fletcher?" I smiled and stuck out my hand.

The man shook his head and gave an embarrassed laugh. "Er, no, ma'am. I'm Larry Hamilton. Bob sends his apologies. There's been a change of plan and he can only spend two days a week with you now. But you're welcome to stay at his place for the weekends. You can have a bath and wash your clothes and Bob can take you back to the Park on Mondays."

My heart sank. Wildwatch had given me lots of information and a training day, but they'd promised an expert would camp with me and explain what the wolves were doing. Now it looked like I'd be on my own for three days a week.

"But will I be safe?" I gulped.

Larry nodded. "Oh sure, plenty of folks camp by themselves."

Larry was still apologizing as we drove through the park entrance. "Thing is, Bob's kinda tied-up. Apart from being our team leader he does talks about wolves to local groups and he's a bit behind on his paperwork..."

Humph, I thought, gazing at the endless forest of lodgepole pines. I couldn't blame Bob for being busy but this sort of thing always seems to happen to me. Being small and mousy, I get overlooked. And because I'm quiet, people think I don't mind. Well, I *do!*

"So what's Bob like?" I asked, trying not to sound too annoyed.

"Bob's ... fine ... once you get to know him, that is. He lives for his job, so you'll be in safe hands."

Yes, for two days a week, I thought bitterly.

Larry was trying to be nice to me. "Say, Willow, would you like to see a geyser?" he asked brightly.

I'd much rather see a wolf expert, I thought, but I nodded. "Sure."

And that's how I visited Castle Rock geyser ... but before I tell you about it I ought to say a bit more about the Park.

WILLOW'S WOLF NOTES
YELLOWSTONE PARK

1. Yellowstone is the oldest National Park in the USA – it was founded in 1872.

2. The Park covers 8,991 square km – that's bigger than the American states of Rhode Island and Delaware put together! It's so big that it takes over a month to walk around it.

3. Yellowstone is famous for its geysers. They're like water volcanoes where boiling steam blasts to the surface. The Park has more geysers than anywhere else on Earth.

4. Amongst the animals that live in the Park are...

ELK

EAGLES

WOLVES

5. When the Park was first set up, the wolves were hunted until they were wiped out. More wolves were brought to Yellowstone from Canada in 1995 and today over 200 wolves live in the area.

We pulled over in a quiet valley. Ahead of us was a rocky rise, dark against the sun. Wisps of steam swirled into the air. I imagined a giant having a bath somewhere deep underground.

Larry glanced at his watch. "The geyser blows every 12 hours. It shouldn't be long now," he announced.

I shuffled my feet and wondered what would happen. I'd never seen a geyser erupt...

Just then, with a mighty WHOOSH! a jet of water roared into the sky. Imagine a huge hot tap blowing up and the billowing steam blotting out the sun. And it went on and on. Unfortunately we didn't have time to hang around, but Larry said that the blast lasts over an hour. I'm camping a long way away from the geysers, but at least I can tell my friends that I've seen one, and I've got this photo to prove it!

Our next task was to head up the Lamar Valley to find a camp site. We drove to a handy lay-by and set off up the grassy slope. I was grateful to Larry for carrying my heavy rucksack and pointing out a good place to pitch my tent.

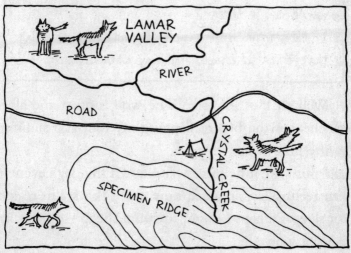

On the way Larry answered my safety worries and gave me some useful tips...

WOLF SAFETY TIPS

1. Wolves rarely attack humans and often avoid us, but it pays to be careful when they're around as:
- An adult wolf can easily kill a human.
- Sick wolves may be more likely to attack.
2. Keep a distance from feeding sites and where there are wolf puppies. The wolves may defend these areas and they'll be upset if you get too close.
3. Never approach a wolf.
4. If you come across a wolf unexpectedly:
- Don't stare. The wolf will think you're a threat.
- If you can, back away slowly. If not, sit down and bow your head. You'll be showing the wolf that you're not a threat.
5. Never run from a wolf. It will chase anything that tries to escape. And may attack you.

Well, that's it for today. The wolf is quiet and all I can hear is the breeze flapping my tent and sighing in the pine trees.

I must say it helps to write down the day's events. I'm feeling less annoyed now and I think I'm ready for sleep. Perhaps I ought to count sheep – or should that be wolves?

May 27

When I opened my eyes this morning I couldn't believe that I was in Yellowstone Park. All of last night's fears had vanished and I felt excited at the start of my big adventure. I wanted to wriggle into my clothes and start exploring straightaway.

I've pitched my tent beside a meadow that slopes down to a creek – that's a type of stream. It was just getting light and I watched the gleaming sun rise over the pine trees on the other side of the creek. But then I began to feel the cold. My breath steamed and my teeth chattered and I longed for a hot bath and hot coffee. Oh well, at least I could manage coffee...

Or so I thought. I soon found out that when you live in a tent even the simplest jobs, like making coffee and breakfast, take quite a lot of planning. Before I could start, I had to trudge to the creek and fill a heavy bucket of water. Then I had to totter back to the tent without spilling too much of it.

I heated a big saucepan of water on my primus stove. This took for ever! And then I needed my coffee and milk and food.

SLOP!

Wildwatch had advised me to store food in a bag up a tree, out of reach of prowling bears. So I had to walk to the tree, untie the rope and lower the bag, then take out my breakfast things and hoist it aloft again. After I'd finished eating, I headed back to the tree, lowered the bag and sent my cooking things back into the branches.

The people who run Yellowstone Park are keen to keep the area free from pollution. After the meal I had to take care not to tip any dirty water near the creek. And I needed to dig a hole when I went to the toilet.

It sounds like I'm a whining whinge-bag, but I'm not, honestly! It's still early days, but I think I'm going to like living in the wild. Maybe it's the calm beauty of the woods, but I've never felt so relaxed.

May 28

Yesterday I was so busy getting used to my new way of life that I only managed a quick stroll around the meadow. But this morning I made up my mind to see what the view looked like from the top of Specimen Ridge.

I picked my way up the slope past clumps of pine trees. Every so often I paused to look for wolves. But I saw nothing and the only sound was the wind in the pine trees and the distant trickling of a creek. The scene had a sense of vastness and emptiness that took my breath away.

At the top of the ridge I turned to look back at the Lamar Valley. From there the river looked like a shiny ribbon and I could see distant mountains with patchy snow on their tops. Further up the valley I glimpsed lines of black dots plodding over the hillside. I guessed they were elk. Maybe the wolves were hunting them, but I couldn't see any...

THE LAMAR VALLEY

This evening, the big, round moon shone like a pearl in the black starry sky. I sat in front of my tent and gazed happily at the moonlit meadow. Could a ghostly grey wolf be lurking in the inky shadows? Tomorrow I'll be meeting Mr Busy Bob Fletcher. I wonder if he can find the wolves?

MEETING BOB

May 29

Well, I've had the pleasure of meeting Mr Robert Fletcher at last. NOT. I'm sorry to say that Bob and I get on like fire and water.

HELP!

Today I hung about the camp site waiting for him all morning. When I finally saw the distant figure I felt like waving my arms like a castaway on a desert island. It's only been a couple of days but it seemed like I hadn't seen another human for ages.

Bob has dark eyes and a sprinkling of grey in his neatly parted dark hair. He has a bristly moustache, a strong chin and a piercing glance that misses nothing.

When he grasped my hand, he stared at me. I felt as if I was being inspected.

BOB FLETCHER

"Hi, I'm Bob Fletcher. How's it going?" he said.

"Um, OK," I replied.

"Great, now here's what we'll do. It's too late to go looking for wolves today, so I'll pitch my tent and we'll try tomorrow. Make sure you're up at dawn."

Bob was used to giving orders. I didn't like it – I'm not used to being ordered about. I tried to help with his tent but got tangled up in the guy ropes.

"I guess you haven't camped much, huh?" sighed Bob. "Have you ever seen a wolf in the wild?"

I shook my head. "Er, no."

"Well, just try to do as I say, right? Otherwise I can't guarantee your safety."

"I do know a bit about wolf safety..." I began.

Bob stopped and stared at me. "Willow," he snapped. "I'm not too sure if you know anything right now. You're in the wild for the first time. For all I know you're an accident waiting to happen."

I gasped and looked away. I hate people who make me feel small! Not surprisingly we didn't speak too much this evening, and I went to bed early.

May 30

Bob was up before sunrise. "Hey, are you awake in there?" he called, smacking the top of my tent.

"OK, OK," I groaned. "I'm getting up!"

It would have been OK if Bob had left it at that. But he didn't.

"Hurry up," he snapped. "We gotta get moving to find the wolves."

I peered dozily at my watch. Bob was right, I'd overslept, but I wasn't going to say sorry.

Half an hour later we were on our way. Bob had made himself coffee without offering me any. He strode on ahead grumbling about this not being a summer-camp vacation. I puffed after him muttering that I knew very well I wasn't on holiday.

THINGS TO TAKE WOLF-WATCHING
Binoculars
High-power telescope
Camera

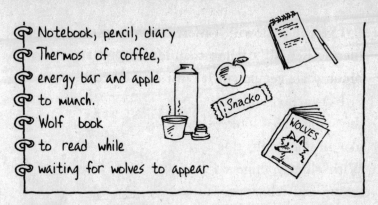

Notebook, pencil, diary
Thermos of coffee,
energy bar and apple
to munch.
Wolf book
to read while
waiting for wolves to appear

Bob was carrying a box of equipment and something that looked like a TV aerial. About half a kilometre from the camp site he suddenly stopped in the middle of a meadow.

"This equipment is a radio receiver," he announced as I caught up with him. "The aerial picks up a signal from a radio collar that I put on the female wolf last year. The receiver shows the wolf's direction and distance. Now, I need you to hold the aerial while I try to get a fix on her."

I held the aerial up as high as I could, which wasn't that high as I'm not very tall.

"OH DANG!" complained Bob. "Hold it steady. I got a fix just then, but you lost it!"

"I'm doing my best!" I protested.

Bob took off his headphones. "She's up on that ridge," he said, pointing. "Let's go take a look."

I guess Bob doesn't know how to say thank you. We set off across the meadow and up a wooded slope.

"Sssh! Get down!" ordered Bob, lowering himself silently behind a fallen tree. He tugged at my arm. "Hurry up, get down! It's just over there."

I crouched and saw the wolf. He looked like an enormous dog. With clumsy fingers I set up my telescope. I took in his pricked-up ears and slanting amber eyes. I could see every hair on his silvery-grey coat and the black nose perched on his snout like a lump of coal.

MY FIRST WOLF!

My heart quickened. At last – my first wild wolf! This is what I'd come to Yellowstone to see.

I stared, fascinated, at the beautiful creature, wondering what he would do next. Had he seen us?

Who's afraid of the big, bad wolf? I said to myself half seriously. His big feet were all the better to chase me with and his big teeth were all the better to eat me with... But the wolf didn't look bad, he looked, well, happy! He wagged his tail and his mouth opened to show a pink drooling tongue.

Just then a second wolf bounded out of the forest. This one was smaller and jet black with a blue radio collar around her neck. She jumped on the bigger wolf as if trying to wrap her paws around him.

"That's the female," whispered Bob. "The bigger wolf is her mate. What we've got here is the alpha pair − the leaders of the pack, which is only them, and their pups. There's two other packs in the Lamar Valley but this is the smallest and so they're easier to study. Hey, are you going to write this in your diary?"

To be honest I hadn't written anything. I'd been too busy watching the wolves.

"Duke," I said quietly. "That's what I'll call him − he's got a lordly look. And the female has to be … Duchess, that's the name for a duke's wife."

Bob gave me a pained look. "I prefer numbers. It's more scientific."

I ignored him and watched the wolves through my telescope. Duke and Duchess bounded around each other, chasing and tearing about like a couple of puppies. At last they lay down wagging their tails happily and gazing at each other with affection. The big bad wolf image popped like a balloon. Well, I always knew it was rubbish. It's hard to imagine this loving couple gobbling up a granny.

Just then Bob tapped my shoulder and pointed to some bushes about 50 metres further up the slope. There stood the scruffiest wolf I'd ever seen. He was smaller than the others and his straggly off-white and grey fur looked like an old mop.

"That's their yearling – a kind of teenage wolf," said Bob. "He was born last year with a brother and sister, but they wandered off in the spring."

As we watched, the new wolf trotted forward a few paces. He had a rather clumsy way of walking, as if he was just about to trip over his own paws. Seeing the other wolves, he crouched and let out a feeble whimper. He seemed especially scared of Duke.

"I think I'll call him Scrappy," I said. It sounded a good name for such a scruffy wolf.

MY FIRST SIGHT OF SCRAPPY

Duke stood watching Scrappy with his tail up and his mouth open. Screwing up all his courage, Scrappy moved forward to lick Duke's nose. But the top dog took no notice of Scrappy as he loftily allowed him this favour. Bob told me that licking the top wolf's nose is a wolf greeting. After a bit more nose licking from Scrappy, all three wolves silently turned and trotted off amongst the trees.

"So what do you think?" asked Bob.

"They're beautiful," I said with feeling. "But they're not as wild as I expected."

Bob tutted. "Huh – that what all tourists say! They figure wolves have got to be chewing up elk every second. But wolves are family creatures – they've got a caring side."

I took a deep breath. I'm NOT a tourist, Bob! I wanted to shout. In fact I didn't say anything – but sooner or later I'm going to put him right!

June 1

I'm glad I didn't argue – knowing Bob, he'd have lost his temper. And then I'd never have stayed at Bob's house this weekend and made friends with his wife, Anne, and his children, 12-year-old Matt, and six-year-old Ellie. I like Anne and I get on fine with Bob's children.

When we arrived, Anne welcomed me at the door. "Hi, Willow," she smiled. "It's good to meet you!"

BOB'S FAMILY

Bob's large bungalow is so clean it shines. I felt like a tramp turning up in dirty clothes clutching a whiffy bag of washing. But no one minded. I sleep in a comfy guest room that Anne calls my home from home and I've got my own bathroom for a much-needed hot soak.

Everything was fine until last night when Bob and I were talking in his study. Bob's study is his own space. Anne doesn't clean in there and it's piled high with wolf books and wildlife magazines.

"So which wolf are you going to write about? I guess you're waiting to see the pups?" said Bob leaning back in his black leather chair.

"Well, actually I was thinking of Scrappy," I said.

Bob's face fell. "*Scrappy?* But he's a yearling. If he left the pack like his brother and sister, he might prove hard to find."

"But he'll be more interesting than a pup. He's old enough to go hunting," I objected.

Bob sighed. "He's also old enough to go missing."

"But I *like* Scrappy," I said obstinately.

Bob shrugged. "Go on then, I guess it is your diary... But there's one more thing," he added. "You've got a lot to learn about wolves and I don't want you watching them alone next week."

"*What?* But that's why I'm here!" I protested.

"We'll go wolf-watching together on Thursday. But until you've got more experience I don't want you taking any stupid risks."

So that's it. I'm allowed to write about Scrappy but I'm not trusted to see him most days! I felt ready to chew Bob's curtains, and I retreated to my room to write up some wolf notes.

WILLOW'S WOLF NOTES
WOLF BASICS

1. All wolves are members of the canid family, a group of animals that includes foxes, coyotes and, surprise, surprise – dogs!

2. There are two main types (or species) of wolves, the red wolf and the grey wolf...

• Red wolves live wild in only a few parts of the USA. They're smaller than grey wolves and reddish in colour.

• Despite their name, grey wolves can be brownish, black, white or a mixture of these.

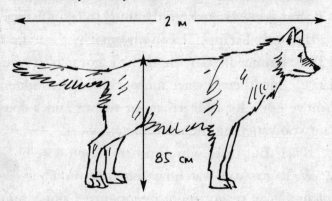

3. Grey wolves once lived across North America, Europe and Asia but humans have wiped them out in many places.

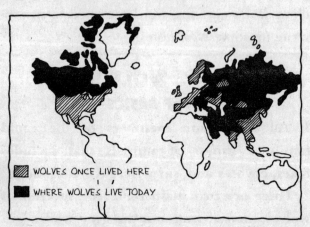

WOLVES ONCE LIVED HERE
WHERE WOLVES LIVE TODAY

4. Wolves usually live in the open, but their pups live in a hole in the ground called a den.

June 2

Ever since I saw Scrappy I've wanted to tell you more about him. So I've combined some wolf-pup info from my wolf book with a few things Bob told me last week to tell Scrappy's story, as he might have written it!

My life so far by Scrappy

I was born last year in the den where Mum's new puppies live. I had a brother and a sister and when we were little, we all curled up with Mum at night.

After a few weeks my brother and sister began to pick on me. They chewed my tail and bit my bottom and stole my food. But I didn't mind – I'm an easy-going wolf. Just so long as I get a few scraps, I can put up with anything!

CHEW, CHEW!

When we were four months' old, Mum and Dad took us hunting – not to take part, of course. Our job was to watch and learn all we could. After the first snows, we began to hunt properly but I still haven't caught anything on my own!

Last winter, we all went hungry and dreamt of big juicy elk steaks. My brother and sister wanted to hunt for themselves and one spring day they just wandered off. But I wasn't brave enough to follow them. At least I get fed here, even though Mum and Dad get cross and growl at me now and then.

SCRAPPY

Today I've made a plan. On Friday I marked on the map where Bob and I saw the wolves. Tomorrow I'm going back there. Yes, I'll be ignoring Mr Bossy-boots Bob Fletcher's orders, but I'm sure I can watch wolves safely! Wish me luck and I'll tell you how I get on!

June 3

I struggled up the slope with my heart pounding. At last I was going wolf-watching on my own! Behind me the misty Lamar Valley glowed pink in the rising sun. It was going to be a lovely morning...

After a bit of confusion and tripping over tree roots I managed to find the fallen tree trunk we had crouched behind. The hillside was quiet and empty, but I felt sure the wolves were nearby. I settled down to wait for them. Waiting can seem a long time when you don't know how long you'll be waiting.

As the minutes went by, I began to wonder if the wolves were further up the slope, so I crept forward another 300 metres to take cover behind another tree. Just then I saw the wolf. He was only ten metres to my right and he didn't look too pleased.

I went cold. It was Duke! I must be too close to his den. The big wolf snarled and I saw his sharp white teeth. My heart stopped. THIS IS BAD, I panicked. I had to get away – but how? If I ran, Duke was sure to attack...

THE WOLF PUPPIES

June 4

Last night I couldn't finish telling you what happened when I met Duke. My torch batteries ran out and I was plunged into darkness! I heaved a cross sigh and put away my diary until the morning.

As I was saying ... things looked bad. My heart was pounding and I thought I was going to die – but suddenly I remembered the wolf safety tips. Duke wanted to defend his den. But if I could show I wasn't a threat, maybe he wouldn't attack.

I took a deep breath and slowly, *very slowly*, I shuffled round on my bottom to face the wolf. Then I bent my head and sat trying to look pathetic. It was hard – at any moment I expected to feel the wolf's jaws around my neck.

I'm Scrappy, I said to myself. I'm a harmless little wolf – p-l-e-a-s-e don't hurt me! But would it work?

Suddenly Duke growled and turned away. I gasped with relief as he trotted up the slope back to the den. It was time for me to leave, and I backed away on wobbly legs. Maybe wolf-watching is more dangerous than I thought!

June 5

Bob is back and I've decided not to tell him about meeting Duke on Tuesday. He'll tell me off for disturbing the pack. He might even ban me from wolf-watching altogether!

NO WOLF-WATCHING!

Today Bob led me to the den on a roundabout route involving lots of scrambling up steep hillsides, bog squelching and bush beating. And he didn't even think of slowing down as I struggled to keep up with his long strides. At last, muddy and scratched, I puffed my way to the top of the ridge to find Bob scanning the scene below through his binoculars.

"There's the entrance," he said.

I couldn't see it, but we were about 500 metres above the place where I'd met Duke. So I was right – the den *had been* close by.

"Can't we get a bit nearer?" I asked.

Bob gave me the sort of look a teacher gives to a kid who asks a stupid question.

"No," he said firmly. "There's a risk the wolves might abandon the den if we get too close."

Hmm, I thought, biting my lip, just as well I didn't tell Bob about my little adventure!

Just then Bob spotted the wolves. "We'd better get behind the ridge," he said.

I followed Bob to a lichen-covered rock and began to set up my telescope.

"It's just the adults. No sign of the pups," reported Bob as he gazed through his binoculars.

Eagerly I peered through my telescope and all at once I saw the wolves. They were locked in a play fight, rolling in a muddle of whirling paws and furry bodies. A moment later, Duke was on his feet, chasing Duchess in ever bigger circles until he caught her and nipped her backside. I couldn't believe my eyes. Here were two grown wolves acting like kids – I mean puppies. Just imagine if human adults did this!

GRRRRR!

Bob was less surprised. "Play behaviour is common between adult wolves," he said dryly. "It reinforces the bonds between the alpha pair."

All very scientific, Bob, I thought. But I bet they play for FUN!

As Bob was talking, Duchess was busily licking Duke's face. Duke looked away and a moment later the female wolf vanished! I was just puzzling over this when Duchess returned. Behind her toddled three fluffy bundles with pinprick ears and stumpy tails. Of course! She's fetched the pups, I thought. The den must be hidden in a dip in the slope.

WILLOW'S WOLF NOTES
PUPS AND DENS

1. Wolf pups grow for 63 days inside their mum and they're born at the end of April. There can be up to six pups in a litter.

2. The den is usually dug by the mother wolf, but it can be a cave or even a hollow log. Dens are often reused every year and some dens are hundreds of years old!

3. The pups are born blind and deaf. All they can do is drink their mum's milk and snuggle close to her for warmth. For the first four weeks, she stays with the pups and the other wolves bring her food.

4. After a week, the pups can hear and about a week later they can see properly. Even so, it takes another three weeks before the pups are ready to stick their heads outside the den. This is an exciting moment. The other wolves can't wait to sniff and lick the pups and welcome them to the pack. Within a few days the mother wolf will go off to hunt leaving the pups in the care of a "babysitter" wolf.

5. The pups grow fast. They can put on over 1.3 kg a week and after a year they're nearly as big as an adult wolf. Imagine if humans did that!

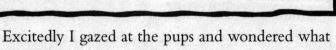

Excitedly I gazed at the pups and wondered what to call them...

One pup had a brown-red patch on his head and as I watched he tried to climb on top of his sister. I'll call him Rusty, I thought. It's more or less the colour of his head. And the pup he's climbing on is a bit dusty – so I'll call her Dusty. But what about the other pup? He lay with his nose on his little paws, tired out after a long, hard snooze in the den. I'll call him Dozy, I decided. He looks rather sleepy!

As I was choosing the pups' names, Dozy struggled to his feet, gave a little yawn and scampered over to his brother and sister. With a yelp of triumph he threw himself on top of them and wriggled his way to the top of a furry puppy pyramid.

ARENT THEY CUTE!

I just wanted say "Ahhhh". These weren't killer creatures, they were bouncing babies with fuzzy little legs and clumpy little paws. "They look just like puppies!" I exclaimed.

I expected Bob to tell me off for being unscientific, but he nodded. "There's something in that," he admitted. "After all a dog is a kind of wolf."

"Really?" I asked. I knew dogs and wolves were related but surely they weren't the same?

Bob nodded. "Yeah, really. Dogs don't look like wolves because they've been bred to look different. And dogs act differently. They're less fierce and they mate twice a year instead of once a year for wolves."

My Auntie Gertrude has a yappy little poodle named Fifi. I tried to picture Fifi as a slobber-dripping wolf, but somehow I couldn't.

June 6

Today Bob had a surprise up his sleeve.

"You wanted to get close to wolves. Well, I've found a way to do just that..."

"What's that?" I felt taken aback. It was Friday and we were supposed to be heading back for the weekend.

"Just pick up your rucksack and follow me," said Bob mysteriously. He clearly didn't want to spoil his little surprise.

Bob led me through a forest, across a stream and a meadow. At last, when I felt totally lost – there it was. A chain-link fence forming a big circle in the forest. Bob dumped his rucksack and peered at the fence through his binoculars.

"What is it?" I asked, laying down my rucksack.

"Holding pen," replied Bob. "It's for problem wolves to cool their paws after going places they shouldn't. See that fella over there – he's one."

I gazed through my binoculars at a shaggy black wolf that was pacing up and down just inside the chain-link fence.

"Number 362," said Bob. "He killed a rancher's dog in Custer National Forest."

NUMBER 362

We walked up to the fence and I gazed at the wolf in the pen. The wolf stopped pacing and looked back at me with dark, sad eyes. He had a ruff of long black hair around his neck and a white splotch on his nose.

"Ahhh, isn't he lovely? What's going to happen to him?" I asked.

"Number 362 came from a pack near Nez Perce Creek. Next week we'll take him back and hopefully he'll stay there."

"And if he doesn't?"

Bob sucked in his breath. "Then he's even more of a problem than we thought. We'll have to use lethal control."

"You mean, he'll be shot!" I burst out.

"It's policy," said Bob harshly. "It's what we have to do and there's no sense in getting emotional about it."

I nearly punched him. I'm NOT emotional! Well I am, but it's better than being a cold-hearted scientist who kills wolves because they're in the wrong place!

I turned my back on Bob and gazed fondly at Number 362. "Just take care," I whispered. "Stay out of trouble, *please*."

June 9

It's Monday and here I am back at the camp site after a much-needed weekend break. Bob seems to look forward to the weekend too. As soon as he walks up his garden path he turns from Dr Wolfman the bossy scientist into Mr Devoted Dad, always ready to play baseball with Matt and cuddle Ellie. It's a side of him I don't see much of when we're alone.

June 11

If only I could go wolf-watching! I thought this morning as I mooched about the meadow. Maybe I could go to the rock and see the den. I felt sure I would be all right now I'd been there with Bob. But if Bob found out I'd be in such big trouble I didn't want to risk it. It's s-o-o frustrating!

In the end I didn't go. I found something interesting to write about at the end of the meadow. It was a wolf scat (or poo). And I almost trod in it!

I expect you'll make a face and say GROSS! when you read this, but don't be put off. It showed the wolves were marking their territory (the area they hunt in).

WILLOW'S WOLF NOTES
WOLF TERRITORY

1. Wolf territories can be anywhere between 65 and 2,500 square km. The territory has to contain enough prey animals to feed the pack, so the fewer prey there are, the bigger the territory needs to be. By the way "prey" means the animals wolves hunt.

2. Besides howling to warn off other wolves, the pack uses wee and poo to mark the borders and vital landmarks of their territory.

3. The smell of the wee and poo tells other wolves who made it and how long ago.

4. Dogs are doing the same thing when they leave little doggie messages at lampposts. No wonder other dogs are so interested in sniffing these places!

Territory is vital for our pack. Last Friday when we were going back in the pick-up, Bob told me there's a big pack of about 20 wolves just to the west of here. He reckons there'll be trouble if they ever have bad hunting.

"What sort of trouble?" I asked Bob, thinking that I wouldn't like the answer.

"Could be anything. Could be a bit of snarling at the border or a full-scale attack. They could kill our wolves in order to hunt in their territory."

"That's terrible!" I said, wondering how Bob could be so calm about it.

"It happens," Bob shrugged. "And the other pack are ruthless – they're led by a big female and she's a real tough lady. She killed one of her sisters for daring to challenge her."

Let's hope the neighbouring pack has good hunting!

June 12

Bob's back and at last I can see the wolves again. Today was wet and drizzly and the trek up to the den was especially muddy. When I finally squelched and puffed my way to the ridge Bob was on his second cup of coffee.

"You could do with more exercise," he observed.

Well, it would help if I were allowed up here more often, I thought crossly.

All was quiet at the den and we could see Duchess lying on guard at the entrance. Then, after a few minutes she lifted her head and howled softly. I held my breath, and listened hard. Yes, there it was! An answering howl. It told us Duke and Scrappy were back from the hunt...

By now the pups were squeaking with excitement at the prospect of juicy meat. But when Duke and Scrappy appeared, their heads were bowed and their tails drooped. The hunt had failed – there was no supper for the pups.

Desperately the pups threw themselves at the adults' mouths, nipping and licking and whimpering and begging. At last Scrappy drew back, shook off Rusty and slunk over to a pile of stones a few metres away. He bent his head and began to sniff the place. Carefully, he began to dig.

I couldn't work out what Scrappy was up to until I saw him pull out a strip of manky meat. It looked vile and I'm sure it smelled worse. Bob guessed Scrappy had buried it some time before – wolves do this if they've got too much meat to eat in one go.

YUM YUM!

But Scrappy wasn't going to be left in peace. The pups dashed over to their older brother and began nipping at his mouth. Scrappy snarled rather weakly. But he made the mistake of dropping the meat and in a few seconds it was torn to bits by the slobbering, scuffling pups. For them every meal is fast food and the meat vanished more or less instantly.

Scruffy watched in dismay as his supper was eaten in front of his eyes. I guess I'd have felt the same if Class 5 scoffed my sandwiches!

June 13

This morning Bob dragged me out of bed extra early and we set off before dawn. I must say, I'm getting better at waking up at strange times in the morning! As the first rays of the rising sun shone across the valley, the wolves began to stir. Duke lifted his head and sniffed the air. He stood up stiffly, stretched like a cat and had a morning wee. Then, fully woken up, he set off to wake Scrappy.

DUKE STRETCHING

Scrappy was fast asleep under a bush.

He dragged himself to his feet and gazed around in a dozy daze. Then he remembered his lowly place in life and he cringed before Duke.

"Morning, Dad," he seemed to whine. "Sorry I didn't grovel just then – I'm still half asleep."

Scrappy wagged his tail timidly and snuffled Duke's nose. But Duke ignored his son. He lifted his head and closed his eyes. His mouth opened as if in a giant yawn and he howled. Scrappy joined in.

WILLOW'S WOLF NOTES
HOWLING AND OTHER WOLF SOUNDS

1. Wolves howl:
• To find other members of the pack if they get separated.
• To make the pack feel like a team before they go hunting.
• To warn other wolves to stay away from their territory.
2. Wolf howls can be heard over 16 km away. When a pack starts howling, neighbouring packs often howl back.

3. Wolves howl at different notes to fool other wolves their pack is bigger than it is. It's all part of frightening other wolves away.

4. Besides howling, wolves growl or snarl when they're angry, whimper when they beg and bark to give a warning.

Duke's voice had a gruff tone, but Scrappy's howl was a pathetic reedy whine. When Duchess heard the calls, she scrambled out of the den to join the chorus. Soon all the wolves were howling together in the cold morning air. For the wolves, the howl was a big thrill and soon they were so excited they started playing run and chase, and their yelps brought the pups piling out of the den to join in the fun.

June 18

Something is up with the wolves. Most nights I only hear the odd howl, but this week they've been at it for hours. They've even woken me up with their high calls echoing on the breeze.

So what's going on? I'll have to ask Bob to be sure, but my guess is that the big pack is moving into our pack's territory. The howls are the warning calls of both sides. If I'm right this could spell big trouble.

June 19

I wanted to tell Bob about the howling, but before I could open my mouth, Bob had news for me. What he said drove wolf howls right out of my head.

"I'm sorry, Willow, I've got some bad news."

"W–what bad news?" I stammered.

"It's Number 362. You know you asked about him last week?"

I nodded. Bob had told me that the wolf had been set free as planned.

"Well, he turned up on a ranch again. I'm afraid he had to be put down. There was nothing we could do."

"Of *course* there was!" I said fiercely. "You could have given him another chance."

Bob sighed. "You don't understand. We have to look after *all* the wolves in our area. We need the support of the ranchers around here…"

"Never mind the ranchers – what about the wolves?" I snapped.

I stalked off in the direction of the forest. I didn't know where I was going. I just knew I had to be alone for a while. I stumbled blindly through the forest to the next meadow ... and stopped dead.

I could see wolves – lots of them. How many were there? Luckily, my binoculars were around my neck. I held them tightly to my eyes, trying to make sense of the scene. The wolves were in two groups. The three wolves closer to me were ... Duke, Duchess and Scrappy. And who were the other wolves bunched together, growling and snarling with fierce eyes? They must be some of the big pack.

The biggest of these wolves was a huge grey female. The black markings around her eyes and nose made her face look like a skull. She bared her teeth in a snarl and spit dripped from her jaws.

THE BIG PACK

Duke and Duchess stood watching the rival wolves. Their tails were up and they didn't seem about to run. But Scrappy was scared out of his wits. His eyes were dark and his ears were back and his scruffy fur seemed to be sticking up in terror. He didn't know whether to back off or stand his ground.

OUR WOLVES ARE IN DANGER

Slowly Duke and Duchess turned and began to edge away. They were still tense. Every so often they turned to glare at the other wolves. But Scrappy didn't move. He seemed rooted to the spot as the big female stalked angrily towards him. A moment later she charged, bounding over the rough grass with terrible speed. Scrappy turned to flee but it was too late. He had no chance of escape.

HOW I LEARNT TO HOWL

June 21

Last night I didn't want to write any more. I was too upset to go over what happened. But I've got to tell you. It's important…

I didn't think. I just stood up and shouted, "LEAVE HIM ALONE!"

I hate the thought of a big bully picking on a weaker person, and that goes for wolves too. At that second I wasn't scared – I was raging.

I tore into the meadow waving my arms furiously. "BACK OFF!" I screamed. "LEAVE HIM ALONE!"

Now the wolves had seen me, there was no turning back. Suddenly I felt scared. These were killer dogs. They could destroy me with ease.

Duke and Duchess were already moving off and Scrappy put his head down and ran towards the safety of the forest. But the big pack just stared at me and growled and bared their teeth. And then, with my heart pounding and my breath gasping I saw something out of the corner of my eye. A splash of red.

It was Bob. He marched out of the forest about a hundred paces ahead of me waving two big sticks.

"YAAAAAAAAAH!" he yelled.

At the sight of two humans, the big wolf leader paused and turned and that was the signal for the other wolves to back off. Suddenly they were all trotting away. I stopped to watch them, tears running down the inside of my glasses.

Bob ran over to me. "WHAT WERE YOU UP TO?" he demanded.

I turned to look at him. The tears were coming faster. "I was trying to save Scrappy!" I wailed.

"You could've got yourself killed!"

"So what!" I sobbed. "Someone's got to care about saving wolves rather than killing them!"

Bob put his hands on my arms and looked at me. "Listen," he said. "I care about wolves as much as you do. To be honest, that's why I agreed to look after you – I wanted to do some wolf-watching away from the office. And, OK, I wasn't too happy when I heard you had no experience of wolves. I figured you'd be after a free vacation writing big bad wolf stories..."

"No way!" I declared fiercely. "I'm not interested in fairy tales. I want to show what wolves are really like. OK, so I'm no expert, but I want to learn."

"I know that now," said Bob softly.

By now we were walking back towards the camp site. "Look, I feel I've been kinda hard on you, not letting you watch wolves on your own. From now on, you can, just as long as you stay behind the ridge near the den – OK? And no more heroics..."

I dried my eyes. "OK, I promise," I sniffed. "And thank you, Bob."

Well, that was all yesterday. This morning Bob and I went to check on the wolves. And they were fine! It was as if the showdown had never happened. The pups were happily playing their favourite games. Rusty was chasing his tail, and Dusty and Dozy were wrestling and snarling and pretending to be fierce. In the middle of them all sat Scrappy. He was watching the pups, trying to keep some sort of order.

Suddenly Rusty grew tired of chasing his tail. With a cunning wolf-puppy grin, he crept up behind

Scrappy. He gave a small yelp of triumph as he bit his brother's backside and scampered off. Poor Scrappy! He's got the naughtiest little brothers and sister in the whole wolf world!

HEE HEE!

By the end of the afternoon I felt things were better between Bob and myself. OK, so Bob has his little ways – he still orders me about and sometimes he snaps at me. But today he made a big effort to be nice. He waited for me when we walked to the den and offered me coffee from his Thermos.

I think Mr Fletcher and I are starting to get on...

June 23

I woke up this morning feeling good. Today I'd be watching wolves on my own, with Bob's blessing! At long last I'll be able to tell you what Scrappy's up to every day. Well, that was the plan...

This morning, the windy hillside where I watched the pups play was empty. And by the afternoon, I was sure of it: the wolves had gone.

GONE AWAY

I sat there miserably, with the chilly wind flapping the hood of my waterproof and whistling in my ears. My eyes watered. It might have been tears.

Where were the wolves? I wondered. Had there been a fight with the big pack? At last I could stand it no longer. Despite my promise to stay behind the ridge, I knew I had to take a closer look.

Slowly, I stood up and picked my way down the rocky slope. Every so often I stopped and looked around me for the wolves, but there was no sign of them. Nervously, I bent down and peered into the dark, earthy-smelling den. All was quiet. The den was empty. The wolves had definitely gone.

June 24

The rain woke me up. It was clattering on the roof of my tent in cold, wet sheets. All I could do was huddle inside and hope it would ease off. I waited and waited and it wasn't until the afternoon that the rain turned to watery sunshine and a rainbow. At last I could go and look for the wolves.

Once again I found nothing at the den, but as I was making my way back to the camp site I came across marks in the soil near the creek. Wolf tracks. I stared at the tracks with new hope. Perhaps Duke had come this way. But where did they lead?

I followed the tracks up the slope. They didn't go in a straight line but wandered into bushes as if the wolf was pausing to sniff scents. It was odd, but following a wolf's footsteps made me feel closer to the wolf. I felt as if I was walking with the wolf even though he was no longer there.

WOLF TRACK

"OH NO!" I groaned. Suddenly the tracks disappeared. The ground had become rocky and Duke must have scampered over the rocks and moved off in another direction.

With a sigh, I wandered across the rocks, widening my search in circles, but I couldn't find any more wolf tracks. At last, with muddy boots and wet trousers, I made my way back to the tent. Was this something to do with the big pack? Were our wolves lying low? I wondered. I haven't heard a howl for days. Could this be the end of my diary?

June 25

Today there was more rain. I passed the time writing these depressing notes about the dangers for wolves...

WILLOW'S WOLF NOTES
IT'S A TOUGH LIFE FOR A WOLF

1. One in two wolf pups die in their first year and few wild wolves live beyond 12 years.

2. Some wolves are killed by other packs in fights over territory. A few wolves are killed by members of their own pack, but this is very rare.

3. Wolves can be killed by bears or the large animals they hunt – elk, moose or bison. In some countries, human hunters are the biggest killers of all.

— YIKES!

4. Wolves suffer from dog diseases such as rabies and canine distemper. They can also get worms from eating the flesh of sick animals. As the worms multiply, the wolves weaken and they can starve to death.

5. In the winter, avalanches and drowning after falling through thin ice are also major killers.

Bob turned up at lunchtime. Before he could even put up his tent, I was pestering him with questions. Where were the wolves? Had there been a fight with the big pack? Were they hiding?

Bob held up his hand. "OK, OK! I'm not too sure right now. Let's go and check out the den for clues."

The den was as empty as it had been on Monday. Then Bob slapped his forehead. "Jeez, I should have guessed!" he exclaimed. "The pups are about eight weeks old now. It's common for pups to be moved about this time."

"Moved!" I squeaked in a relieved voice. "So it's nothing to do with the other pack?"

Bob shrugged. "I can't say they didn't hurry things along. But my guess is that the wolves were ready to move anyhow."

OH, THANK YOU, BOB! I thought, and I nearly hugged him!

"The pity is," continued Bob, "I don't have my radio-tracking gear to find them this week. But there's one thing we could do..."

"What's that?"

"We could howl."

"*Howl?*"

"Yeah, I'm not keen on it because it gets the wolves worked up. But at least we could check out if they're nearby."

Bob stood up and took a few deep breaths, then his head tipped back and he cupped his mouth with his hands. His mouth yawned open and out came an amazing sound...

"*Aooooooooo-ahhhhh-ahhhh!*" Higher and lower it went. I gazed at Bob in astonishment. It was as if there was a wolf standing where he was.

BOB HOWLING

Suddenly Bob stopped and listened intently, cupping his ear. Only the breeze answered him.

"Hey, why don't you try?" offered Bob. "I'll show you how it's done."

HOW TO HOWL LIKE A WOLF

1. Take a couple of deep breaths.
2. Lift your head back and cup your hands around your mouth.
3. Howl. Try to make your howl rise and fall slowly and try to keep it going for a few seconds.
4. If you're howling with friends, try to make sure your howling note is different to theirs.
5. Once you've got the hang of howling, try waggling your tongue as you howl to get differing notes. Wolves do this if they're real singing stars!

"*Ooooh-ahhhhh-oooooo!*" I wailed. I sounded like Scooby Doo with toothache.

"Very good!" encouraged Bob. He cupped his hands, lifted his head and howled again.

We howled together.

Suddenly my spine tingled. I heard a sound. *Ooooooh!* A real wolf howl! As we listened, more and more wolf voices joined in. I felt thrilled to hear the wolves answering us in their own language.

I gazed around, trying to work out where the howls were coming from, but it seemed to be nowhere and everywhere at once. Again and again the wolves' song rang out from some lonely, distant hillside.

June 30

These days I feel at home at Bob's. Anne greets me with a hug and then Matt and Ellie come up and ask me to help with their homework. This weekend all the talk centred around the coming 4th July holiday. Anne and Ellie will be at a birthday party, but Bob and Matt are looking forward to a trip to the Park.

Breathlessly Matt told me their plans...

"We're gonna stay at your camp site for a night – if it's OK with you. Dad says we can look for wolves."

July 1

I've just seen a wolf! Probably. Twenty minutes ago I was cooking noodles for supper. I looked up and glimpsed a dark shape amongst the trees across the creek. My heart stopped. *Was it a wolf?* It was hard to see anything against the glare of the evening sun.

"Don't go away!" I whispered urgently. I rummaged in my bag for my binoculars, but by the time I found them, the creature had gone.

So what was it? Could it have been Scrappy? I'm making a special wish to see him tomorrow...

THE WOLF SCHOOL

July 2

HUH! So much for wishes! I haven't seen a whisker of a wolf today. And to be honest, I think I imagined seeing Scrappy yesterday. So what's going on? Are the wolves avoiding me? Their senses are sharp enough to tell them where I am. And maybe we upset them by howling. Maybe they think *we're* a rival wolf pack?

July 4

Bob and Matt turned up at the camp site in time for lunch. They were carrying rucksacks and Bob had brought his radio-tracking equipment.

"I just can't wait to have a go with that direction finder," Matt was saying. "It sounds real neat."

"OK, son, let's get our tents up first." Bob smiled. "Then I'll fix us something to eat. You hungry, Willow?"

I nodded. Living out in the open makes me hungry all the time.

Later

The wolves' new home turned out to be a hidden valley with a stream trickling through it. The valley had thick bushes at one end, but it was overlooked by a low rocky ridge which was ideal for wolf-watching. From it we could see the wolf tracks in the soft ground, the boulders where the pups were playing, and the well-chewed bones of old kills.

"That," said Bob, "is what we call a rendezvous site – it means meeting in French. It's a kind of wolf school. A meeting place where the pups can practise hunting but still be fairly safe."

WOLF SCHOOL

"So how long do they hang out here?" asked Matt, his eye glued to my telescope.

"Until about mid-September — by then they'll be old enough to travel and hunt with their parents."

A shadow passed over the pups. Bob looked up with a sudden frown.

"Hey, what's going on?" broke in Matt.

Looking up, I saw an eagle gliding across the empty sky. Scrappy scampered about, barking excitedly. Duchess raised her head, scanning the sky, and the pups huddled in terror.

"Is it going to attack?" asked Matt.

"I shouldn't think so," said Bob evenly. "But you never know."

As the shadow moved off the pups began to relax. In a few minutes they were racing across the valley as if nothing had happened. It was one more alarm in a life full of excitement.

July 7

Today I've been finding out about how wolves can tell each other where they stand in the pack pecking order. Take a look at this photo...

Duke is very much the wolf in charge. See how he stands tall with his tail up and his ears forward. He's looking straight at Scrappy to show that he's the top dog. And Scrappy is grovelling with his tail between his legs and his ears flat. He doesn't dare look at his dad. A moment after I took this picture, Scrappy rolled onto his back and showed his tummy. It's the wolf way of saying, "YOU'RE THE BOSS!"

These actions are vital. To stay alive in a tough world the wolves have to hunt as a team and each wolf needs to know its place. And it's not just wolves that make these actions – dogs do it too! When your dog wants feeding it whines and tries to lick you. And that's how the weaker wolves beg for food.

LICK
SLURP!

July 8

Watching the wolves today made me realize that a wolf's face shows how it's feeling. In this way, they are just like us, except that wolves don't make silly faces to amuse their friends.

Take Scrappy, for example. Today my wolf looked rather pleased with himself as he welcomed Duke and Duchess back from hunting. But when Scrappy tried to grab the pups' supper, Duke turned on him with an angry look and Scrappy cringed away with a really scaredy-wolf expression on his face!

This evening I had a giggle practising wolf faces in my pocket mirror.

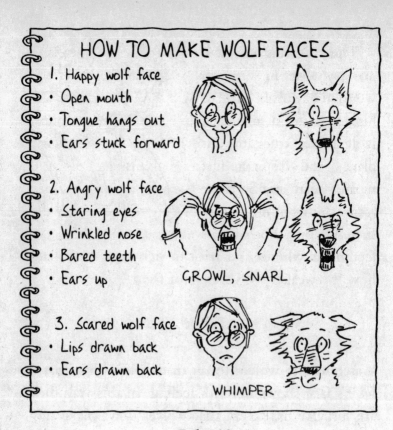

HOW TO MAKE WOLF FACES

1. Happy wolf face
   • Open mouth
   • Tongue hangs out
   • Ears stuck forward

2. Angry wolf face
   • Staring eyes
   • Wrinkled nose
   • Bared teeth
   • Ears up

GROWL, SNARL

3. Scared wolf face
   • Lips drawn back
   • Ears drawn back

WHIMPER

July 10

Honestly! All the time I've been telling you about wolf faces, I've been missing something important happening in front of my very nose! Bob pointed it out this afternoon.

"Hey, Willow, have you noticed? Scrappy's having a hard time with the pups."

"But Scrappy's always having a hard time with the pups," I shrugged.

"He's having an even harder time today," said Bob.

Bob was right. Today will go down in pack history as the day Scrappy lost control of the pups. It all began when the pups were racing along the bank of the stream. Suddenly Rusty dipped his head in the stream and began to slurp up the water. Dozy joined him, but Dusty was sniffing the grass near the stream. Her tail began to wag with excitement.

"Looks like she's found something," remarked Bob. "Could be a leftover scrap or a dead mouse."

It must have been a tasty morsel. A moment later all the pups were snarling and scrabbling to get at it. Scrappy, who had been resting at the top of the slope, trotted down to join them, but Rusty raised his head and gave a fierce snarl.

"TAKE A HIKE, SCRUFFBALL – WE FOUND IT!" he seemed to warn.

Scrappy stopped dead. His mouth opened, his eyes widened and his tail thwacked. Then he turned, visibly upset, and backed off. At the top of the rise, Scrappy stopped and turned back to look at the pups. He raised his head and let out a soft, sad howl.

"Hear that?" said Bob. "Scrappy's calling the pups."

Hearing the howl, the pups stopped feeding and looked at Scrappy. Then, all together, they lifted their heads and howled back at their brother. But that's all – they wouldn't budge from the stream, and after a while Scrappy crept into the bushes by himself.

"WOW!" said Bob. "You've just seen Scrappy lose face to the pups big-time! In a few days, he could be the underdog for them, too."

July 11

Do you know what? I think it's summer! All this week I've been dabbing myself with mosquito repellent to get rid of the annoying mini-vampires as the hot sun climbs into the blue sky. Bob says that this is the hottest Yellowstone ever gets.

"Some folk say that Yellowstone has summer in July and winter the rest of the year," he joked.

The wolves are also feeling the heat. Today they lazed in the shade of the rocks, panting and snoozing and longing for the cooling breeze of dusk.

For a few weeks the wolves have been shedding their thick winter coats and every so often one of them rolls in the dirt to rub away some more hot, unwanted fur. In places the ground is so littered with hair that it looks like a wolf hairdressing salon. Scrappy's hair is as tufty as thistledown. He looks like a sort of bedraggled sheep – or at least a wolf in sheep's clothing!

And so the afternoon passed until, just as we were making ready to leave, Bob spotted something.

"Willow, look over there!" he said tensely.

I pointed my telescope at the bushes at the end of the valley. And that's when I saw it... A big brown lumpy shape topped with a pair of round furry ears.

My mouth dropped open. Whatever it was, it was BIG. "Is that a...?" I began.

"Yeah," agreed Bob in a low voice. "A grizzly bear. I'd say it's a male, and it's hungry."

BEWARE OF THE BEAR

The wolves had also spotted the bear. Duke bared his teeth and glared at the big beast with dark, angry eyes. Duchess gave a worried bark and, as if by magic, the pups vanished into some bushes. Meanwhile, Scrappy was cowering and wondering whether he ought to hide in the bushes with the pups. What would the bear do? All the wolves waited anxiously.

"This looks bad," muttered Bob.

"What do you mean?" I hissed.

"The bear wants to eat the pups. If the wolves fight back the bear could kill them all."

"NO!" I gasped in horror. And just then, the bear charged...

WOLF DINNERS

July 12

We spent yesterday evening at Bob's house telling
Anne and the kids the story of the bear attack. In fact
I was so busy talking about the drama that I didn't
have time to finish my diary.

When the bear charged, I expected the wolves to
run. But they stood their ground, snarling fiercely.
The bear slowed to a walk. He was growling and
swinging his huge head furiously as he tried to scare
the wolves from the den. His massive muscles rippled
under his shaggy coat. Even on all fours, the bear was
as tall as me – to the wolves he must have looked like
a huge, hairy elephant with killer claws and teeth.

Scrappy slunk away in terror. "So sorry, nothing
personal, I'll be on my way," I imagined him whining.

Duke was made of sterner stuff. Silently, he slipped round behind the bear and then he darted forward and bit the bear's backside.

The bear was startled. He swung around, lifting a huge paw to swat Duke, but the quick wolf dodged the blow. And then it was Duchess's turn to sink her teeth into the bear's behind. Once more the bear turned and this time Duke ran at him. With a snarl and growl the bear reared up on his hind legs, beating the air with his forepaws. Then he sat down and gave the wolves an evil look.

It was a stand-off. The bear glared at the wolves and the wolves glared back at the bear. Every so often the wolves pretended to creep forward. They were keeping the bear busy, and protecting their pups. At last, the sun dipped behind the clouds, and the bear decided to call it a day. With a final angry grunt he lumbered off into the twilight.

AND DON'T COME BACK!

"I think it's gonna be OK," whispered Bob.

I sighed with relief. In nature, life is as exciting and dangerous as a soap opera. But there's a difference – when a character dies, they die for real.

July 16

I sat watching the valley for two hours this morning with a rising sense of panic. The wolves weren't at the meeting place. What if the bear had paid them another visit?

At last, when I could bear the suspense no longer, I decided to circle the area in search of tracks. And that's when I found the body. All I could see was a collection of bloody ribs sticking up above the tall grass on the edge of the meadow. A couple of ravens were busily ripping strips of meat from the bones and you could hear the flies buzzing excitedly round the manky meat.

Was it a wolf? I panicked. No, it was an elk. The wolves had been feeding on the body and it was so close to the meeting place that the pups had been allowed to feed too. The wolves were probably resting nearby after their meal, so this wasn't a good spot to hang around.

Suddenly the ravens cawed in protest and flapped away. The hairs on the back of my neck stuck up. Something's coming, I thought, and nervously I headed up the slope. It proved to be a wise move. As I glanced back, the wolves appeared from the forest.

July 17

Bob was over the moon about the elk kill. Yesterday his boss asked him to write a report on wolf hunting and feeding habits. Bob needs to know which animals the wolves are eating and whether they eat all the meat. The chance to watch the wolves feeding on the kill was too good to miss.

I led Bob to the kill and half an hour later we found ourselves watching the wolves from the cover of a nearby grassy mound.

Through my telescope I could see the wolves crowding around the elk's body in a mass of yelps and snarls and teeth. But as I looked more carefully, I could see that only Duke was feeding. Hungrily, the big wolf was ripping meat from the body and crunching the bones.

WILLOW'S WOLF NOTES
WOLF DINNERS

1. Do you wolf your dinner? It's a good way to describe wolf table manners because wolves eat as much as they can, as fast as they can. An adult wolf can wolf down about 15 kg of meat in one meal – that's about one third of its bodyweight!

2. But wolves aren't greedy. They eat a lot because they don't know when they'll feed again. It could easily be a week or more and they need to keep their strength up to hunt.

3. Speedy guzzling is vital to ensure the wolf gets its share before the other wolves eat it.

4. The alpha wolves always eat first and generally choose the heart, liver and lungs of the prey. These bits are full of fat and energy and wolves love them.

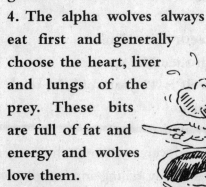

5. Some of the food will get sicked up for the pups. Don't make a face when you read this! A wolf's tummy is a sort of lunch box to store food. The pups love feeding on the sicked-up meat because it's served nice and hot and well mashed-up!

6. Wolf teeth are designed for eating meat...

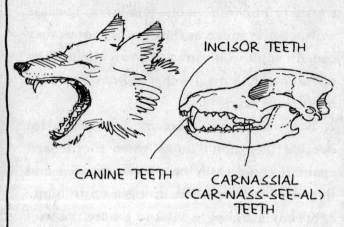

INCISOR TEETH

CANINE TEETH

CARNASSIAL
(CAR-NASS-SEE-AL)
TEETH

• Canine teeth grab meat and are used for hunting.
• Front incisor teeth rip and tear.
• Carnassial teeth slice like scissors.

By the time a wolf is 12 years old, its teeth are blunt and worn.

The other wolves were waiting their turn. Duchess was standing and watching and Scrappy was tearing around in circles at the back of the queue.

Meanwhile the pups were jostling the adults' legs, with their tails wagging and their mouths drooling.

DINNER TIME

At last Duke was full up and it was Duchess's turn to grab her share. As Duke turned away from the meat, Scrappy saw a chance to get in his dad's good books. Timidly he crept up and offered to lick the blood off his jaws. But Duke shook him off and trotted to the stream for a drink. Rejected, Scrappy crouched with his head on his paws.

Scrappy was so busy feeling sorry for himself that he didn't see Duchess letting the pups nip in and grab some choice titbits from the feast.

"See that?" asked Bob, as we watched the pups feed with excited yelps and playful snarls. "Looks like Scrappy's fallen down the pecking order. He's a real omega now!"

"An *omega*?"

"That's the bottom wolf in the pack. Omegas get picked on by everyone and they have to feed on scraps."

Scrappy by name and scraps for his supper, I thought sadly.

"So why does there have to be an omega wolf?" I asked.

"Someone's got to be bottom of the pile. Omega wolves are there for the other wolves to take out their bad temper on. All they can do is start games to keep the other wolves in a good mood..."

ANYONE FANCY A GAME?

Poor Scrappy! I didn't tell Bob, but as a kid I was a bit of an omega. I was the one with glasses who sat at the front of the class because no one wanted to sit with her. I had no friends or brothers and sisters and I spent my spare time playing with my pet dog and pretending he was a wolf.

July 24

Bob turned up this afternoon in a good mood.

"I've managed to get hold of our most up-to-date radio-tracking device," he explained proudly. "And that means we've got a great chance of following a wolf hunt!"

A wolf hunt! Now that sounded exciting!

"It's a hard thing to do," added Bob. "Wolves can cover over 50 kilometres when hunting, but as long as they don't run behind any hills we can follow them in the pick-up. I figure we'll see some action!"

But that'll be tomorrow's story...

July 25

This morning we had to pack up our tents in the dark. Bob said that we had to be on the move before dawn in order to catch up with the wolves before they made a kill.

I was still yawning and rubbing my eyes as we set off towards the end of the valley. Twice Bob parked the pick-up in lay-bys and set off up small hills to get a radio fix on Duchess. At the top of each hill, he lifted the aerial in the air on the end of a pole and listened for signals, but each time Duchess was still a few kilometres ahead of us.

At last, on the third attempt, Bob took off his earphones and laid down the aerial triumphantly.

"We've got them!" he said. He picked up his binoculars and studied a ridge half a kilometre away. "Yeah, look – there they are!"

Through my binoculars I could see the sunlight glittering on the brown coats of the elk herd. And there, flitting like ghosts in the swirling dust around the elks' hooves, were the wolves.

"Yes, I can see them!" I exclaimed. "They look like sheep dogs rounding up the elk."

THE WOLF HUNT

"Not quite," said Bob. "They're trying to chase the elk into smaller groups, and pick out the weakest ones."

I held my breath as Duke and Duchess trotted towards each group of elk, testing them, daring them to scatter. And the elk trotted stiffly away.

"See, the elk are showing the wolves how strong they are," said Bob. "The stiff trot uses a lot of energy. The elk are saying we're fit and healthy, so don't bother chasing us!"

The elks' trick seemed to work because Duke and Duchess turned away and approached another group. But where was Scrappy? Was he testing elk? No, he'd wandered off, his tail swinging with excitement. He was dashing towards a huge elk stag! The stag was far too big for Scrappy to tackle. Had he gone mad?

YEE-HA!

With an angry snort, the big elk galloped off in a cloud of dust and flying hooves. Scrappy seemed scared by the noise and sat down, looking confused. Meanwhile Duke and Duchess were doing the job properly. As we watched, they cut off a female elk from the rest of her group and chased her flat out towards the river.

Again and again the wolves leapt snapping at the elk's sides and legs. Again and again the elk kicked out wildly, but each time she did so, she lost ground.

At last the elk stood gasping on boggy ground and now, like a ragged streak of lightning, Scrappy dashed over – keen to do his bit. Without thinking he threw himself at the elk's side. But the elk saw him and kicked out with her hooves.

"NO, SCRAPPY! NO!" I cried.

Just then, Duke fastened his jaws on the elk's nose and dragged her head to the ground. The elk's hooves kicked wildly in the air. Frantically she pulled herself to her feet, but now Duchess was biting and snapping at her sides and even Scrappy uselessly got hold of her tail. Silently the elk shook her head in a desperate bid to free herself from Duke's grasp, but her strength was gone and she fell back to the ground.

In a few moments the wolves were feeding hungrily. We kept our distance and now the elk was on the ground it was hard to see the bloody details...

"They're quite scary when they hunt," I whispered to Bob.

Bob shook his head. "I don't see it that way. As a scientist I can see the benefit the wolves provide. By taking the weakest elk they keep the herd strong and healthy. Ravens, coyotes and bears eat the wolves' leftovers, and even the birds and beavers do well."

"Birds and beavers?" I frowned.

"Before wolves were brought back to Yellowstone, elk ate most of the young trees. Wolves keep elk numbers down so the young trees have a chance to grow and provide shelter for birds and beavers."

I imagined the Park as a kind of woolly jumper with every animal as a thread. Unpick the wolf thread and everything falls apart...

July 28

After last week's drama my mind was buzzing with questions about how wolves hunt. So this weekend I've dug out a few facts from Bob's wolf books...

WILLOW'S WOLF NOTES
HUNTING HINTS

1. An old Russian proverb says:

A WOLF IS KEPT FED BY ITS FEET

It means that a wolf has to run to catch prey.

2. A wolf can trot all night and all day and still have enough energy to chase an elk at 60 km an hour for a minute.

3. Snow doesn't hold up wolves much. A wolf's toes are webbed so they can spread out

when the wolf walks on them. This makes the wolf's foot larger to support the animal's weight and stop it from sinking into the snow too deeply.

4. Often, wolves sneak up on their prey with the wind in their faces so that the prey can't scent them. Wolves have even been known to roll in rotting fish to mask their smell!

5. Nine out of ten wolf attacks fail and even when the wolves catch their prey, pulling it down is a dangerous job. A maddened moose can kick a wolf 4.5 metres in the air!

July 31

I was hoping that Bob would bring his radio equipment today and we'd see another hunt. But the equipment was needed elsewhere and Bob was after another item for his report. Wolf poo. For a wolf expert, every scat tells a story.

"I'm not kidding," said Bob brightly. "Look at a scat closely, and you can find all sorts of clues to a wolf's lifestyle. There are hairs and bones from its prey, so you can see what a wolf's been eating. And then there are eggs from worms living in its guts..."

I left Bob to his labels and sample boxes and went for a long, long walk. It was a good move. In the late afternoon I caught a glimpse of the wolves returning from a hunt.

Duke and Duchess were there, but Scrappy had been left behind with the pups. I guess he had been more of a hindrance than a help last week.

August 1

While Bob continued to comb the landscape for wolf poo, I watched the meeting place. Once again Scrappy was in charge of the pups, although these days the pups tend to be in charge of Scrappy. After a while Scrappy got bored of being picked on and wandered off down the valley.

At first I wasn't sure where he was going, except that he'd obviously scented something. His head was down amongst the grass and his tail was wagging with excitement. All of a sudden he tore first one way, and then the other, darting backwards and forwards and scattering clods of earth as he went.

What had Scrappy found?

A moment later I saw it. A hare. Of course, it was no contest. The hare jinked and turned, wrong-footing the wolf every time. At last, puffed-out and panting, Scrappy sat down and gazed after the hare as it streaked into the long grass. All he could do was pick himself up and pad miserably back to the pups.

SCRAPPY AND THE HARE

When I told Bob what I'd seen he said, "Hmm," in a rather interested voice. "That figures. Wolves often hunt small animals on their own. For Scrappy, it's a chance to practise his hunting skills, but there's something more..." Bob rubbed his chin uneasily.

"Something more?" I asked.

"Yeah, like now he's an omega, he may not be getting enough to eat."

"You mean the food's going to the pups?"

Bob nodded. "Yeah – as the pups are getting bigger, they eat more. And that means less for Scrappy. I guess he's trying to catch his own supper."

So it wasn't a game! Scrappy was hunting because he was hungry. And he'd failed miserably.

August 5

If Scrappy's hungry it helps to explain the trouble this evening. But it doesn't make it less shocking. It all began innocently enough with a tussle over food after Duke arrived back at the meeting place with food for the pups.

As usual, Scrappy wanted some too. At the sight of the sicked-up meat, the young wolf went crazy. He threw himself at the food, scattering the pups.

All of a sudden, Duke was standing over him with his teeth bared and his tail thrashing. I've never seen him so angry. For a moment I thought the big wolf was going to bite Scrappy's neck. Scrappy thought so too. He gave a frightened bark and backed away, but Duke hadn't finished with him yet. As Scrappy cowered and cringed, Duke lashed out with his heavy front paw and knocked the smaller wolf over.

Scrappy went down as if he'd been punched, and he stayed down, hiding his head in his paws and whimpering. I held my breath and waited, but Scrappy didn't move. Duke glared for a few more moments before turning his back in fury. I'm no expert but one thing is clear. Scrappy can't expect to be fed by the others. From now on, he's on his own...

August 6

This afternoon the weather changed. Storm clouds unrolled over the mountains like grey smoke. The sky grew hot and airless and after sunset it began to rain. The storm had begun.

Later

I'm writing this as the tent bends and shakes in the howling wind and the guy ropes take the strain. It's scary. It feels like my tent could blow away at any second. The pouring rain is turning the meadow into a marsh. I wonder what's happening to the stream? Will the stream flood and sweep the wolves away?

Some time around dawn the wind died down and the rain eased off. As the sun rose, the meadow was wet and glittering and still. It was time to check on the wolves, and as soon as I was dressed I hurried along the muddy track to the meeting place.

Were the wolves OK? Yes! There were Duke and Duchess, playing with the pups as if nothing had happened. But where was Scrappy? The stream was rushing over the boulders at the bottom of the valley and tugging at bushes. Had he been swept away?

I asked Bob when he came at lunchtime.

Bob saw my pale face and smiled. "Hey, Willow, don't worry – he's probably OK! My guess is he left the pack before the storm. It's been on the cards for a while now."

I wasn't convinced. "Can't we just take a look further down the stream to see if he's been washed down? Oh, please, nice kind Bob!" I begged.

Bob's a lot more sympathetic to me these days and in the end he joined me in searching. But we found nothing and tonight I must close my diary with a sad question. What has become of Scrappy?

August 8

Today we made ready to leave for the weekend with the mystery as unsolved as yesterday. But then, just as I was about to get into the pick-up, I spotted something by the Lamar River.

"Look over there!" I cried to Bob. "It's Scrappy. I'm sure of it!"

Bob reached for his binoculars and scanned the meadow. I was right! Scrappy was sitting beside the river, half-hidden in the long grass.

"What's he up to?" I asked Bob.

Suddenly, Scrappy bounded down the bank and leapt into the ugly yellow-brown water...

For a split-second I couldn't believe my eyes. "OH NO! HE'S GOING TO DROWN!" I screamed.

Bob and I dashed through the wet grass to the water's edge and stared at the raging river. But there was no sign of the wolf. Scrappy had gone...

THE WAR AGAINST WOLVES

August 11

When Bob dropped me at the lay-by this morning I was still thinking about Scrappy. I hadn't stopped wondering about him all weekend. Somehow I felt sure that he'd made it. I even dared to hope he might be hanging about on the opposite bank wearing his usual hangdog expression. But the meadow was empty. Scrappy was nowhere to be seen. He wasn't near the camp site or the meeting place, or in the forest. And now the question is whizzing around my head like a hamster in a wheel. Why did Scrappy jump in the river? I think I know the answer...

Scrappy was alone and frightened. He knew he couldn't go back to his pack and he couldn't stay where he was. Perhaps he heard the howls of the big pack in the valley and knew they'd kill him if they found him. He gazed at the river and felt that crossing it was his only chance.

August 13

This week has been a washout for wolf-watching. The rain began on Monday. Not stormy like last week, more of a slow, steady rain that doesn't know when to stop, so it goes on ... and on ... and on.

With nothing better to do, I found myself wondering how Scrappy's senses are going to help him survive on his own and I've made a few notes.

WILLOW'S WOLF NOTES
INCREDIBLE WOLF SENSES

1. Wolves can see at least as well as humans and some experts report that wolves can spot distant prey animals that humans can only make out with binoculars.

THERE IT IS!

WHERE?

2. A wolf's sense of smell is 1,000 times more powerful than ours and they can sniff out prey 2.5 km away.

3. A wolf can hear sounds through 6 km of thick forest or 16 km of open country.

I drifted into a daydream in which I was Scrappy loping through the cold rainy forest. My senses felt ultra-alert and super-sharp. My eagle eyes spotted the tiny twitch of a hare under a faraway bush. My crystal-clear hearing picked up the pitter-patter of a million raindrops. I could hear the soft downward beat of a raven's wing and the faint footsteps of mice. I lowered my cold, wet nose to the ground and scented the elk that passed this way two hours ago. I really felt like a wolf — and I hoped that with senses like these, Scrappy could find food and safety...

August 15

Last night I woke up with my heart thudding and a strange feeling of danger. I rubbed my eyes and groped in the dark for my glasses. There was something outside the tent...

I could hear it moving. Heavy footfalls, deep breathing. Was it Bob? No, I could hear him snoring. There was only one creature bold enough to come sniffing around a tent in the dead of night and my stomach tied in knots at the thought of it. The creature outside just had to be ... THE BEAR! The huge, hungry killer bear!

I listened hard, trying to figure out what the bear was up to. Was it just about to rip open my tent and hook me with its long claws and drag me shrieking into the forest?

OH-ER!

My heart thudded like a jackhammer. Then I heard a CR-A-A-CK! as the creature trod on a stick and my heart nearly leapt into my mouth. I muffled a scream with my pillow.

Crunch, C-R-U-N-C-H, R-I-P! What was that? It didn't sound like a bear. After a while, my curiosity got the better of my fear. Silently, with clumsy fingers, I unzipped the tent. I peeped out nervously ... and then I saw it. Large and lumbering in the darkness, its huge head shadowed against the starlit sky. It was a moose – a massive male moose with enormous antlers!

Phew! My sigh of relief was more like a gasp. I drew my head back inside the tent and lay still, listening to my thudding heart. I must be crazy to get scared by a moose!

In the morning, Bob woke me with a hot cup of coffee. He's been doing this for a few weeks now. "Did you hear any sounds last night?" he asked.

"Yes," I said bravely. "But I wasn't scared – I knew it was only a moose!"

"Well," said Bob with a frown. "I'm not so sure about that. Come and take a look at this."

As soon as I was dressed, Bob led me a few metres across the meadow and pointed to a patch of bare earth. There was a broad but shallow hoof mark left by the moose. But across it lay an even larger print. The unmistakable shape of a bear's paw with the deep gashes left by its big, slashing claws. I often think how wonderful it is to be close to nature, but last night nature got a bit too close!

August 19

This morning the air was full of the lovely scent of pine needles. But it's colder too. Every day it gets light later and there's a feeling that winter's just a whisper away. But who cares about the weather! What I really want to know is *where is Scrappy*?

On Monday I asked Bob this very question.

Bob sucked in through his teeth. "I wouldn't like to say. Young wolves like Scrappy can wander hundreds of kilometres. But no one's reported seeing him."

"Does Scrappy know where he's going?"

"Probably not. Mind you, wolves are smart. They can figure out how to open a door by turning the handle and that's more than a dog can do."

Well, thanks, Bob. Let's just hope Scrappy is smart enough to know what he's doing!

August 21

At last — news of Scrappy. And it's *bad* news. My wolf is still alive, but he's on a ranch just north of the Park ... and he's killed a sheep.

When Bob told me this morning his voice was tense. "I'm sorry, Willow," he said. "I didn't want to have to tell you this."

I bit my lip. "So what happens now?" I asked anxiously.

"Well, it's our policy to go check out the scene to see if a wolf really killed the sheep and suggest a course of action — maybe remove the wolf to the holding pen."

"And who does that?"

Bob shrugged. "Well, us. Me, usually."

"Can I help?" I begged. At least I might get a glimpse of Scrappy. "Pleeease!"

"OK, sure." Bob nodded. "If you really want to."

Oh I do, I do, I DO! I thought. And I sent out a silent message — *please* let Scrappy be all right!

August 22

We drove north out of the park through Gardiner and along the Yellowstone Valley. The road followed the Yellowstone River past Mammoth Hot Springs, where the steam rose in a thick mist from its pools and ledges, but we had no time to stop and look around.

I stared out the window and thought of Scrappy. I knew what had happened. Scrappy was lost and frightened. His belly was empty. He was starving. Then he stumbled across the ranch. Scrappy had never seen anything like it before. When he spotted the fat, fleecy sheep in the field, he thought it was a free supper. So he ate it.

Later

Mr Tom Williams had a lined, weather-beaten face and an equal mixture of brown and silver hair. He wore jeans, a leather jacket and a pained expression...

TOM

"That there wolf killed a valuable sheep," he complained. "And I want paying!"

Bob sighed. We'd seen what was left of Tom's sheep and he was definitely right. There was even a wolf paw print by the body – Scrappy's calling card.

"I seen him myself as bold as anything," Tom growled. "He was eating the sheep in broad daylight! Life's hard enough for us without wolves being a public menace." His voice was thick with anger.

I clenched my fists and gritted my teeth. Zip it, Willow! I thought, leave the talking to Bob.

"There's various devices to protect livestock," suggested Bob. "For example, a simple line of flags can scare wolves away."

"*Flags?* Where am I gonna get flags from?" demanded Tom. "Say, when are you gonna *shoot* that wolf?"

I spluttered a mouthful of coffee and stared at him in horror. Sometimes saying nothing is the hardest thing of all.

August 25

Next week Scrappy will be caught and taken to the holding pen at Crystal Creek. Scrappy has fallen foul of people, but he's not the only wolf to suffer this fate. You won't believe what I've found out!

WILLOW'S WOLF NOTES
THE WAR AGAINST WOLVES

1. Native Americans admired wolves as fellow hunters, but farmers thought differently. They saw wolves as a danger to their livestock and killed wolves without mercy. In Europe, wolves were wiped out in many countries. The last British wolf was shot in 1743.

2. In North America, the war against wolves was even fiercer. Wolves were shot and trapped and poisoned. Their dens were dug up and their pups were cruelly killed. So-called sportsmen even hired planes to shoot wolves from the air.

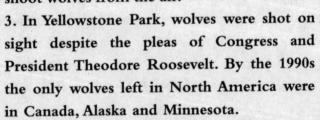

3. In Yellowstone Park, wolves were shot on sight despite the pleas of Congress and President Theodore Roosevelt. By the 1990s the only wolves left in North America were in Canada, Alaska and Minnesota.

4. In all, two million American wolves died at the hands of humans. But not one single human was ever killed by a wolf.

But the most heartbreaking fact of all is that, despite the terrible cruelty they've suffered, wolves can make loving pets. There are even stories of trapped wolves whimpering and wagging their tails as the hunter came to kill them. When I read that I came over all emotional. I laid down my pencil and stared into space as the tears rolled down my cheeks.

"Scrappy," I said, dabbing my eyes. "I promise I'll do anything I can to save you. Anything at all!"

And I really, *really* meant it...

August 27

For the past two days, I've been watching the comings and goings of the pack and I've seen Duke and Duchess leading the pups off in the mornings and back in the evenings. Yes – the pups are old and big enough to go hunting, although I guess they mostly watch the action. Sometimes I can see where the wolves are from the tiny black dots of ravens circling in the cold, blue sky. They're following the elk and waiting for the wolves to make their kill.

August 28

Bob arrived this afternoon with great news. Scrappy has been caught. He's safely in the pen at Crystal Creek!

"YES!" I cried, clapping my hands together.

"Dave's one of the best – a great helicopter pilot," said Bob. "It was a routine capture. Scrappy ran off, but Dave swooped in low – just two metres off the ground. Larry leaned out of the chopper and jabbed Scrappy with a syringe on a pole."

"So Scrappy was knocked out?"

"Yeah, sure, but only for an hour or so – just long enough to get him back to Crystal Creek."

"And he's all right now?"

Bob nodded. "Sure thing – you can see for yourself. I was planning to walk down tomorrow to check him over."

So that's settled. I'll be seeing Scrappy tomorrow and although I feel sad that he's locked up, at least he's safe. And I'll be getting closer to him than ever before. Tomorrow is definitely going to be an exciting day...

August 29

Before we went to the pen, we had to walk to the pick-up to collect two orange plastic boxes of equipment and two large nets. But at last, around lunchtime, we found ourselves outside the chain-link fence. It looked black and unwelcoming against the green of the forest.

"There he is," whispered Bob. He pointed to a forlorn dog-like figure with its nose pressed up against the fence.

"It's like he's waiting for us," I whispered back.

"I don't think so," chuckled Bob. "Larry says he's been sitting there most of the time. Waiting for someone to turn up to feed him, I guess! Well, if you're ready, let's go catch ourselves a wolf!"

Bob had done this before and he'd filled me in on his plan as we walked through the forest. We had to get ourselves into the pen and use the nets to catch Scrappy for a check-up. It sounded easy.

Bob unlocked the gate padlock and we moved our nets and boxes inside. Once we were in, Bob dragged the gate shut so that Scrappy couldn't escape. He opened one of the boxes and drew out a red rug to spread on the ground.

All this time, Scrappy was watching us with interest. His mouth was open, his eyes bright with curiosity. Bob carefully filled a syringe with liquid from a container in the second box. Then, passing me a net, he whispered, "OK, let's go get him!"

My heart rattled inside me. Treading cautiously, I walked towards the wolf. Scrappy looked at me. He placed his head on one side, puzzled. "What's up?" I imagined him asking. A moment later he decided it must be a new game and dashed towards me. As he streaked past, I held up my net and threw myself at him. But I tripped and landed spread-eagled with my face in a clump of grass.

Fortunately Bob was more successful. I heard a yelp from Scrappy and Bob yelled in triumph as the wolf was caught.

"Hey, Willow, give us a hand!" he called.

GOT HIM!

I picked myself up and ran towards Bob, who was crouched over a struggling netted Scrappy. Quickly,

I threw my net over the wolf and Bob jabbed him with the syringe. Five minutes later, Scrappy was quiet although his eyes were still open.

"You can lift your net," said Bob gently.

"Is it safe?" I asked in a small voice. After all these weeks of wolf-watching I felt stunned to be so close to one.

"Oh yeah, he'll be out for at least half an hour."

I gazed into the dark circles of Scrappy's soft amber eyes and the wolf blinked back at me. Timidly, I stroked his soft bristly fur. It had a faint, damp, doggy smell.

"Hey, Willow, can you manage to carry him to the rug?" asked Bob.

I crouched and gathered Scrappy in my arms. He was breathing normally, but he hardly stirred. Staggering under the wolf's weight, I carried him to the rug and, with Bob's help, gently laid him down.

"Now to make him comfortable," said Bob.

He placed a muzzle and a blindfold over Scrappy's head so that the wolf wouldn't feel frightened or try to bite us if he woke up. Over the next half an hour, I learnt a lot about Scrappy.

PUFF PANT!

REPORT ON SCRAPPY

1. Judging by the wear on his teeth, Scrappy is 18 months old. His teeth are in good condition.

2. The best way to weigh a wolf is to place him in a canvas bag and hang this from a weighing scale. Scrappy is underweight for his age. He wasn't getting much food in the pack and he may have lost weight on his trip to the Williams' ranch.

3. Scrappy has no signs of disease. Bob vaccinated him against rabies and gave him an anti-worm pill.

THIS IS SO EMBARRASSING!

4. Scrappy is now sporting a red, rather-girly, radio collar. When he's released we'll be able to keep track of where he is.

As the drug wore off, Scrappy struggled to his feet and gazed around as if to say, "What happened?" Meanwhile Bob dragged the gate shut and secured the padlock. I looked at Scrappy with a new sense of closeness – I'd held my wolf. I won't forget that.

September 2

All this weekend I've had something on my mind. A problem. My job with Wildwatch is due to end next Monday. But how can I finish my diary when Scrappy is penned up and I don't know what will happen to him?

Yesterday I spent Labour Day holiday typing a long email to Wildwatch, begging them to let me stay until Scrappy is safely released. Today I got my answer. They said "yes" – I could stay until the 15th!

September 3

This morning I woke up to a changed landscape. In place of the rustling meadow grass and the sighing lodgepole pines, there was only a cold, white silence.

The grass and the trees were heavy with snow. As I watched, soft flakes began to fall.

"WOW!" I gasped and, feeling like a kid, I dressed in ten seconds and scrambled out of my tent. It felt strange to crunch and slide through the snow to the meeting place. All the familiar landmarks and tracks had disappeared, but I got there in the end. And it was worth it just to get this great photo of the pups!

September 4

Bob was late today, and the later he became the more uptight I felt.

"It's the snow," I said to myself. "He's been held up, but I know he'll be coming soon."

When at last Bob came in sight, trudging up the slope in his snowshoes, I watched him anxiously. Through my binoculars I could see his pale face and his drawn expression. Something had happened...

"I've got to talk to you," Bob said. "Scrappy's escaped from the pen. Larry thinks he might not have closed the gate properly when he fed him yesterday."

"Surely that's not such bad news?" I said. "He won't go far from the food."

Bob sighed and shook his head. "No, I'm afraid it's trouble. Scrappy's eaten the meat and headed off. His tracks lead north. It looks like he's heading back to the Williams' ranch."

"WHAT?" I gasped. If Scrappy went back he would die. His life would end with a bullet in the heart.

THE SNOW GROOMER

September 5

I saw everything in terrible detail. Scrappy was bounding through the snow. A shot rang out. The speeding bullet slammed into him and the wolf dropped down, lifeless. I gazed at Scrappy's body as a little puddle of red blood stained the snow. I could even see the snowflakes on the wolf's still body...

Then I woke with a gasp. For a moment I lay still with my heart jumping and thumping, trying to sort out what was real and what had been a dream.

The truth was bad enough. Scrappy was on the run, and he was heading into danger. But at least Bob has a plan. On Monday we'll be taking a helicopter and trying to follow Scrappy. Hopefully, the radio collar will help us find him. Everything is happening so fast. Yesterday, Bob helped me to pack up my tent and clothes and food for the last time. Now the snow is here, I can't camp any more. But Monday seems a long way off. Oh, why can't it come a bit quicker?

September 8

"Are you ready, Willow?" shouted Bob over the roar of helicopter rotor blades.

I nodded. I'm not very good at bellowing.

Bob gave Dave a thumbs–up sign and the chopper swung around and lifted into the air in a whirl of snow. A moment later we rose above the trees. From my seat next to Bob I could see the river snaking through white meadows and wintry cottonwood trees. It was strange to think that just a few short weeks ago it had been summer down there.

Bob put on a pair of headphones and leant over the display on his radio-tracking machine. Hopefully it would tell us the distance to Scrappy using the signal from his radio collar. Hopefully...

Dave touched the controls and swung the helicopter north to follow Scrappy's trail. We flew over the Lamar Valley and followed Buffalo Creek north through wild, snowy mountains. At last, when our fuel was low and it was time to go back, we got a trace. Scrappy was just 16 km from the ranch and he was on the move. It was the worst possible news and all my excitement at the helicopter ride turned to dust. We MUST stop him! *But how?*

September 10

Bob's phone rang this morning. I've been like a wolf on hot bricks for two days. Every time the phone rings, I jump. It must be news of Scrappy, I think. This time it was. Mr Williams was on the line and he was talking so loudly that I could hear his voice.

He'd seen Scrappy close by the ranch. The wolf had stampeded the cattle and scared the sheep and chased Mr Williams's dog. Mr Williams is not a happy man ... nor is Bob.

For days I've been worrying about this moment. What would Bob decide to do with Scrappy? What would I say if Bob tells me that Scrappy has to be put down? This morning I found out.

"Shut the door," said Bob, as I followed him into the study.

I shut the door and sat down facing him. I could feel my heart pounding.

"Scrappy's had his second chance..." began Bob. "I'm afraid he's got to be dealt with."

"Dealt with?" I repeated. I felt a thrill of horror. I seemed to be falling towards the centre of the Earth.

"It's policy," said Bob flatly. "Look, there's no easy way to say this…"

"Easy way!" I burst out. "It's less easy for Scrappy!"

Bob avoided my furious look. "I know you're upset…"

Then I lost it. All the stress I'd been bottling up for days poured out of me. "I'm not upset – I'm angry!" I raged as the tears stung my eyes. "You said Scrappy's had his chance. But what sort of chance is that? You said he'd have two weeks in the pen, but someone left the gate open and he escaped. How did he know he shouldn't go back to the ranch? He was starving. What's he supposed to do – turn vegetarian?"

VEGIBURGER FOR ME, PLEASE!

"I know how concerned you are," Bob said quietly. "I've seen wolves shot and I don't like it any more than you, but my department…"

"Your department let me write a diary for children," I sniffed. "What sort of diary would it be if my wolf gets shot?"

There was a shocked silence. Bob took a deep breath. "Yeah," he said quietly. "I can see that, and it could be said that by leaving the pen early, Scrappy didn't have enough time to forget the ranch."

I took off my glasses and wiped my eyes. "So?" I asked, taking a ragged breath.

"So I'm gonna stick my neck out..."

"Yes?"

"And give Scrappy one final chance."

"YES! THANK YOU, BOB," I leapt up and wrapped my arms around Bob's neck and planted a snotty kiss on his cheek.

Tomorrow, we're going to drive up to the ranch and set a trap for Scrappy. We'll bring him back to Crystal Creek and get him safely locked up. But let's not party yet – we've still got to catch him!

September 11

Mr Williams met us at his door, stony-faced. "That wolf's gone too far this time," he said. "I guess you're gonna shoot him."

Bob held up his hand. "We were at fault," he admitted. "The wolf got out before he had a chance to forget your ranch. This time we're going to trap him and take him back to the pen and make sure he stays there. And when we do let him go, we'll track him to make sure he doesn't come back. I guarantee you won't be seeing that wolf again."

I gazed at Bob in admiration. He was sticking up for Scrappy and saying all the right things.

Mr Williams nodded slowly. "OK, but you better mean it this time," he growled.

We followed him into the kitchen and he offered us coffee. "Don't get me wrong," he said, filling the kettle. "I don't want to see wolves shot. It's just that there ain't room in this valley for wolves and people. How soon do you think you can catch this wolf?"

Bob shrugged. "I dunno," he said. "It could be an hour or two. It could take longer."

Tom spooned coffee into three mugs. "Look here, I want that wolf outta here as soon as possible. But if it takes a couple of days I'd rather you stay and get a result. I can put you up here if it helps."

I nodded to Bob.

"We'd appreciate that, Mr Williams," said Bob. "Perhaps you can show us where you saw the wolf."

Twenty minutes later we were crunching across the snowy field in the direction of a muddy track.

"I saw him just under this tree," said Tom, his

breath steaming in the cold air. "The dog was acting crazy and I didn't want to get close. See, there's the tracks in the snow."

Bob bent down and examined the prints. "I've got a hunk of deer in the pick-up as bait. If it's OK, I'll set the trap here. And then we'll have to wait."

We stayed the night in the ranch. Before I closed the bedroom curtains, I stood at the window and gazed at the soft flakes of snow falling on the dark trees. And all at once I heard the wolf's lonely howl – *Awwww-oooooo!* Scrappy was all alone in the dark and the snow, and I felt sure he was calling me.

WILLOW, WHERE ARE YOU?

September 13

So much has happened since I last wrote my diary! But let's go back to yesterday morning... At dawn, Bob went to check on the trap. The meat was still there. Scrappy hadn't taken the bait.

"Darn!" cursed Bob.

All we could do now was wait and it wasn't until afternoon that we heard a shrill bark from the forest.

"C'mon, Willow," called Bob, rising and reaching for his net and equipment box. "I think we got him!"

We dashed outside and crunched our way over the soft white snow towards the track. Ahead, something rustled in a snowy bush. It was Scrappy. As we drew near, I could see the hurt in his eyes. It wasn't pain exactly, because Bob had set the trap so it wouldn't close on his leg. It was a wide-eyed, shocked look as if to say, "How could you do this to me?"

"It's for your own good, Scrappy," I whispered.

SCRAPPY IN THE TRAP

Scrappy whimpered and struggled as Bob threw the net over him, but he soon gave up. Perhaps he sensed Bob was trying to help him.

A few minutes later we were trudging back the way we'd come. I was carrying Bob's orange box and net, and Bob was carrying the knocked-out Scrappy. On the back of Bob's pick-up was a large metal box drilled with holes. It was a transport box for wolves. Carefully, Bob opened the metal grille on one side of the box and placed Scrappy inside.

"Let's get moving," said Bob. "It's a fair drive back, and I don't like the look of the weather."

And so we said our goodbyes to Mr Williams and bounced off along the road. It had started to snow...

After two hours the snow eased off but it had begun to get dark and the driving was as tricky as ever.

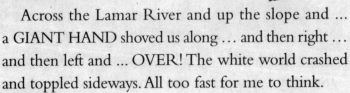

DARN!

"DARN – I can't get a grip on the road!" cursed Bob as we narrowly missed a snowdrift. On we shuddered and slid...

Across the Lamar River and up the slope and ... a GIANT HAND shoved us along ... and then right ... and then left and ... OVER! The white world crashed and toppled sideways. All too fast for me to think.

Darkness. No lights. I was on my side. The pick-up had tipped sideways. I was squashing Bob. He was still – was he dead? No, he was breathing. There was no blood. He must have banged his head. We needed help. Bob's radio! I reached out my hand and touched it. But I knew it was no good, the radio was broken and silent. There was no chance of calling for help.

I had to get out. Clumsily, I unclipped my seat belt. I braced my feet on Bob's seat to push open the door. Then I jumped down, dropping on my hands and knees in the snow. I struggled to my feet and freezing air slapped my face. I stamped my feet to keep warm. I could freeze to death out here, I thought.

And just then, I heard it, echoing across the valley. A wolf's howl. A moment later, other wolf voices joined in. From inside the box that was still strapped to the back of the pick-up, there came a scrabbling noise, and then, *Aaah-oooo!* A feeble answering howl.

THUMP! Scrappy was upset and desperate to get out. THUMP! THUMP! He bashed his body against the sides of the box. I had to give him his freedom. I knew it was the right thing to do.

"OK," I called to Scrappy. "I'm coming, hang on in there."

With shaking hands, I slid back the metal bolt of the grille and lifted it open. I stepped back and the wolf sprang from the box. He thudded onto the snow and scampered off. But only a short way. Suddenly, he turned and swung back, trotting past me and the pick-up in the opposite direction.

"WHERE ARE YOU GOING?" I called.

And then I realized. He was heading towards the Buffalo trail and Tom Williams's ranch. My mouth gaped in horror. Scrappy was going to his death...

"COME BACK – PLEASE!" I yelled.

Again Scrappy gazed at me. His tail wagged.

"Follow me," he seemed to be saying.

Feeling like an elephant on an ice rink, I stumbled after the wolf. But each time I drew near, Scrappy bounded away, leading me on. Clumsily, I trod in the holes in the snow made by the wolf's quick feet and I remembered how I'd followed Duke's tracks.

FOLLOW ME!

Once again I was walking with a wolf, but this time I felt closer to him than ever before. The wolf was leading me, guiding me into the unknown. I was too cold to think clearly. If I'd been thinking straight, I'd never have left the pick-up.

On and on I stumbled, until distance had no meaning and my hands and feet were numb. All at once, Scrappy swerved to the right and began to scamper through the deep, white snow of the meadow. He was heading for the Lamar River. And this time he didn't look back. I knew I couldn't go any further, I was too tired to follow him. If I closed my eyes I wouldn't open them again...

And that's when I heard the sound. A low hum, like a giant bee. What was it? I was still puzzling when I saw the creature's yellow eyes and black face. It *was* a bee – a bee that growled and hummed and stared with eyes of yellow fire. A machine.

"Say, are you lost?" called a voice.

"Help!" I heard someone call in my own voice. "I've been in an accident."

His name was Sam and he saved my life, and Bob's. During the winter snows, Sam drives his snow groomer four nights a week. The machine flattens the snow, so it's safe to drive on. Tonight, Sam happened to be driving this way. It was luck.

SAM AND THE SNOW GROOMER

Sam wrapped me in a blanket and set me up beside him. Then he radioed for help to rescue Bob. I gratefully drank some hot coffee from Sam's

Thermos and thought about Scrappy. Why did he lead me towards the snow groomer? Surely he'd heard the sound before I did? Was that luck too?

September 14

They kept Bob and me overnight for observation. The doctor said that I had hypothermia and Bob had mild concussion. By yesterday morning we were both feeling a lot better. I told Bob that I'd let Scrappy go.

"It's OK," he said softly. "If Scrappy was in danger of getting hurt in the box, you did the right thing."

September 15

Today I went for a drive with the entire Fletcher family. I'm leaving tomorrow and Anne wanted to let me see the Lamar Valley one last time.

"What are those folks looking at?" said Matt as we passed a line of cars parked by the side of the road. People milled around the cars talking and pointing.

"Looks like they've spotted wolves," said Bob.

The excitement tingled through my body. "Wolves!" I burst out. "Can we stop to see them?"

"Sure," smiled Anne, and pulled the pick-up over.

I leapt out. Eagerly I fumbled for my binoculars. And there on top of the ridge I spotted a grey wolf stalking a line of elk. The wolf was strong and powerful — an alpha wolf. My hands were shaking as I gazed at them.

"I think it's Duke," I gasped. "Yes, there's Duchess behind him. And that's..." I stopped and rubbed my eyes and looked again. Yes — a small, scruffy figure trotted along behind Duchess. A skinny wolf with a shaggy coat. "Bob, look!" I cried in a trembling voice. "It's Scrappy — he's back with the pack!"

SCRAPPY'S BACK!

Bob stared in amazement. "Well, who would have thought it? So he's back with his folks. I don't suppose he'll stay."

"But it's OK, he's safe," I said softly.

As we watched, the elk and wolves disappeared over the ridge. But those few moments by the road, in the snow, were my most precious memory of all...

WILLOW'S PRESENT

April 8

Last month Anne phoned to invite me back to the States for the Easter holidays. I should have known something was afoot from the excitement in her voice.

"Do come, Willow," she said. "Your room is all ready and Bob and the kids would love to see you."

"Are you sure?" I asked, feeling secretly delighted.

"Absolutely," said Anne. "After what you did for Bob, we'd love to have you! So do come, say yes!"

I did say yes. To be honest I didn't need much persuading. In the six months since I'd left Yellowstone I'd missed them all terribly.

When Bob picked me up at Jackson Airport there was a twinkle in his eye and a smile on his face. As I said, I should have known that I was in for a surprise.

"I can't promise you any wolf-watching," said Bob. "The snows this year are real bad."

"Don't worry," I assured him. "This time I really am on holiday!"

An hour later we pulled up at Bob's house.

"I'll take your bags," offered Bob. "You go on in."

Anne gave me a welcoming hug before leading me into the living room. "Sit down," she said. "Make yourself at home. I hope you're hungry, I've baked a special cake. Ellie, Matt, can you bring in the food?"

"Food?" I said. "I hope you haven't gone to any trouble just for me."

"Oh no," said Bob. "Not just for you... Hey, guys, you can come in now!"

With a broad grin Bob ushered in his colleague, Larry, Sam, the snow-groomer driver, and Dave, the helicopter pilot.

"And now," said Bob. "Larry's got something for you. A small thank-you gift from us all."

Larry handed me a large, flat present wrapped in silvery paper.

"For me?" I squeaked. "I'll sit down to open it!"

Everyone was looking at me. Matt and Ellie were standing beside me with big grins on their faces.

"We hope you like it," said Anne. She exchanged a knowing smile with Bob. Feeling as excited as a two-year-old, I tore open the rustling paper. It was a picture. A framed photo of two wolves in the snow.

MY WOLF PHOTO

One wolf looked like Scrappy – he even had a red radio collar! But this wolf was different. He was bigger and stronger. Close beside him was a wolf with lovely silvery-grey fur and dark ears and I felt sure that I'd never seen her before.

"Thank you, it's beautiful," I smiled. "You know, it's funny – but that wolf reminds me of Scrappy."

Bob and Anne looked at each other and laughed.

"That wolf *is* Scrappy!" said Matt.

"NEVER!" I gasped.

"Scrappy left the pack early in October," said Bob. "I kinda guessed he would want to be off again as soon as he could. For a few weeks we were all worried because we couldn't get a radio fix on him."

"We thought something bad had happened..." added Larry.

"Bob didn't want to tell you until he had some definite news," said Anne.

"And then, just last month, Larry saw him and grabbed this photo," said Bob. "He was up on the Mirror Plateau with a female wolf. It looks like Scrappy's gotten himself a girlfriend!"

I gazed at the photo again. Scrappy *had* changed! He wasn't just larger – he looked bolder and more powerful. In the past few months he had turned into an adult wolf. Suddenly I had a lump in my throat.

"Oh my goodness!" I sniffed, as big happy tears dripped on the glass. "He's just ... so ... handsome!"

"Looks like he had a good winter," said Bob. "A lot of elk have starved in the snow and I figure they've been easier to catch."

I dried my eyes and looked again at the photo. All at once I could imagine Scrappy's future. He would become a fearless alpha wolf. He would have a loving she-wolf to keep him company and a pack of playful puppies to look after.

"We knew it would mean a lot to you," said Anne.

"Yes," I said, holding the picture tightly. "It means more than I can say. But most of all it means that every day, I'll look at this picture and remember the magic. The sheer wonderful thrill of walking with wolves!"